This
Ladybird Picture Book
belongs to

....

Published by Ladybird Books Ltd
A Penguin Company
Penguin Books Ltd, 80 Strand, London WC2R 0RL, UK
Penguin Books Australia Ltd, 707 Collins Street, Melbourne, Victoria 3008, Australia.
Penguin Group (NZ) 67 Apollo Drive, Rosedale, North Shore 0632, New Zealand

001

Text © Joan Stimson MCMXCVII

Illustration © Ladybird Books Ltd MCMXCVII

First published by Ladybird Books Ltd MCMXCVII

This edition MMXIII

ISBN: 978-0-71819-322-5

Printed in China

Ladybird Picture Books

Worried

Arthur

The Big Match

Written by Joan Stimson

Illustrated by Jan Lewis

Arthur was a penguin and a worrier.

He knew that often he was *over*-anxious, but, if ever he tried anything new...

or exciting...

Arthur *always* worried.

One afternoon, Arthur tore in from school like a tornado.

"Dad! Dad!" he shouted. "There's a letter from my teacher."

"Whatever does it say, Arthur?" asked Dad in surprise.
"I do hope you've not been misbehaving."

"Oh, no!" cried Arthur. "It's nothing like that."
And then he showed Dad the note.

PER ARDUA

AD

ANTARCTICA

Dear Parent,

Your son has been chosen to play for Ice Cap West in the Schools' Five-a-Side Football Final. Please make sure he turns up at 2 o'clock on Saturday with a clean shirt!

Yours Sincerely,

[signature]

Head Teacher

P.S. The Final will be played at this school against last year's winners, Ice Cap East - otherwise known as the Catapults.

Dad read the note carefully and smiled.
Then he read it again and beamed.

"Well done, Arthur!" he cried. "That's splendid news!"

But Arthur wasn't sure.

"What if I let the side down, Dad? I've only been picked because Flip's pulled a flipper," he explained. "And I haven't had half as much practice as Ben, or Katie, or Wally."

"DON'T WORRY, ARTHUR!" boomed Dad. "I've every confidence in your ability. And furthermore," he went on, "I can give you some useful tips myself."

Over the next few days, Dad and Arthur went into training.

Dad built a special practice net outside. And each evening, at supper, he described the exciting goals he'd scored as a young football star.

With each practice session, Arthur improved in leaps and bounces.

But one night, he woke up in a panic and called for Dad.

"Oh, Dad!" wailed Arthur. "I've just had a horrible nightmare. I dreamt I headed the ball into the wrong goal. What if I do that in the Big Match and we lose the final?"

"Arthur," said Dad, firmly, "there's absolutely no reason for you to flip the ball into the wrong goal. Just do your best and I know I'll be proud of you."

"Even if we lose?" whispered Arthur.

"Even if you lose TEN NIL!" Dad told him.

The evening before the Big Match,
Dad ironed Arthur's team shirt.

Next morning, he cooked Arthur's favourite breakfast.
But Arthur wasn't hungry.

"I've got jittery flippers," he whispered.

"I expect you have," said Dad, kindly.
"But fortunately," he smiled, "I have
the perfect cure for jittery flippers."

And before Arthur could ask any
questions, Dad fetched the model
boat he'd been making.

Dad and Arthur spent the rest of the morning by the seashore.
Arthur began to feel better.

"I think I might manage a light snack," he announced at lunchtime.

After they'd eaten, Arthur put on his team shirt.
Dad went to get ready, too. But, when they met
up on the landing, Arthur shrieked with horror.

"Oh, no!" he cried. "You can't come
to the match dressed like that!"

All the way to school, Arthur kept stopping to argue.

"At least leave the megaphone behind," he begged.

But, when they reached the football pitch, they found that other parents were trying out *their* megaphones.

By now, the visiting penguins had begun warming up. The home players were waiting impatiently for Arthur.

"GOOD LUCK, SON!" boomed Dad.

And Arthur sped on to the pitch.

Both teams were on top form.
And, although Katie scored a
BRILLIANT goal for Ice Cap
West... the Catapults bounced
back with a real SIZZLER.

The score was still one goal each
with two minutes left to play.

"West is best! West is best!" roared
the home supporters.

"CAT-A-PULTS! CAT-A-PULTS!"
chanted the visitors even louder.

Arthur was almost exhausted.
"What if I get cramp?" he worried.

Just at that moment, Wally gave the ball
a huge wallop. BOING! The ball bounced
off Ben's beak straight at Arthur's feet.

BIFF! Somehow Arthur gave the ball his best shot.
And THWACK! It landed smack in the Catapult's goal.

PEEEEP! went the referee's whistle.
The Big Match was over.
Ice Cap West had won!

That evening, Arthur had a long soak in the bath.
And at supper it was *his* turn to talk tactics.

But, by bedtime, Arthur was looking worried again.

"Dad," he whispered. "Do you think the Catapults
minded losing?"

"I'm sure they were disappointed," said Dad. "But then,"
he reminded Arthur, "the Catapults did win the final
last year. And, of course," he teased, "I expect they'll
win again next year."

"Oh no, they won't!" cried Arthur. And he bounded out of bed to demonstrate...

another winning GOAL!

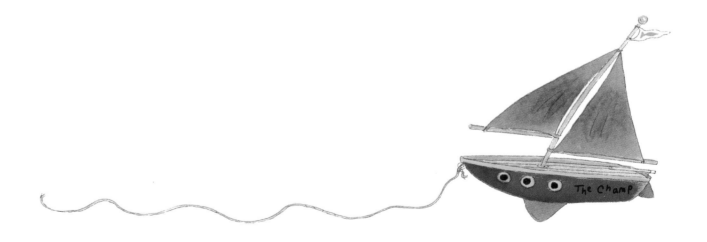